For Tiziana Pirotta – S.G.

Text copyright © Sam Godwin 2001
Illustrations copyright © Stephen Player 2001
Book copyright © Wayland 2001

Published in Great Britain in 2001
by Hodder Wayland, an imprint of
Hodder Children's Books

Re-issued in 2008 by Wayland

The right of Sam Godwin to be identified as the
author and Stephen Player as the illustrator of this Work
has been asserted by them in accordance with the
Copyright, Designs and Patents Act 1988

British Library Cataloguing in Publication Data

Godwin, Sam
  Welcome to the waxworks. – (Tremors)
  1. Horror tales 2. Children's stories
  I. Title
  823.9'14 [J]

ISBN: 978 0 7502 5418 2

Printed in China

Hachette Children's Books
338 Euston Road, London NW1 3BH
Wayland is a divison of Hachette Children's Books,
www.hachettelivre.co.uk

Welcome to the Waxworks

SAM GODWIN

Illustrated by Stephen Player

WAYLAND

Chapter One

Becky stood on the pier, trying to shelter
from the wind under a tattered metal canopy.
The whole of the pier seemed to be rusted.
It needs a good lick of paint, Becky thought.

She looked around her bitterly, as she had done every half-term holiday since her parents had split up. There was the stall that sold hamburgers and candyfloss. And next to it was the fortune-teller's caravan that always seemed to be closed.

Becky's teacher's words echoed in her head: *"I want you to keep a diary of the week. Write down anything interesting that happens to you…"*

It was all right for Miss Cushing. She was off to Spain for the week. Becky was stuck in boring old Skipton, with nothing exciting to do.

A hand came down on Becky's shoulder, making her jump.

"Are you OK, kiddo?" It was Becky's dad. He was the security manager at the pier. "Hope you're not bored already," he said.

Becky grasped his hand and smiled, genuinely pleased to be with him.

"We've got a new attraction," he said proudly. "Waxworks."

"You mean like Madam Tussaud's in London?"

"Not quite as grand," laughed her dad, "but it is one of the oldest waxworks exhibitions in the world. Want a sneak preview?"

"Why not?" said Becky.

Her father led the way beyond the fortune-teller's caravan. "Here we are," he said, stopping outside a huge wooden building. "Perhaps you can write about the waxworks in your diary."

Becky thought he had a point. Waxworks were a bit more exciting than hanging around on the pier. But it was going to take a lot of imagination to make them *really* interesting...

Chapter Two

Friday Night, 8.00 pm

I've just come back from seeing the
waxworks. The first part of the exhibition
was more or less what I'd expected: pop stars
and other celebrities who didn't quite look
like the people they were meant to be. There
was also a historical section, which was just
a lot of kings and queens lined up on a
platform. I could only recognize Henry VIII
because he was surrounded by his six wives.

Then Dad pushed aside a heavy curtain and we stepped through a short tunnel into the Chamber of Horrors. I didn't think much of it at first. There was an executioner by the doorway, welcoming us in. Behind him, on a raised platform, a group of ancient Egyptians were mummifying a princess. One of them was putting her heart in a clay jar. Further away in the gloom, I could see a queen kneeling at a chopping block.

"Mary, Queen of Scots," Dad explained.

The last exhibit was a group scene. A tableau, my father called it. It showed eight children playing in a rat-infested street.

You could tell it was on the outskirts of London because there was the outline of Saint Paul's Cathedral in the distance. These waxworks were much older than the ones in the front room. Their waxy skin was pock-marked with age but their eyes were surprisingly bright and made them look almost alive. I half expected one or two of them to speak.

One of the kids, a stick-thin boy with blonde hair, was lying on the floor. He had a posy of colourless flowers pressed to his chest. His shirt was tattered, leaving his hollow belly exposed. The others were dancing around him. Or were they trying to kick the boy? I wasn't sure. Certainly, they seemed to be sneering, their eyes full of hate. Poor boy, why wasn't anyone helping him?

Behind the kids, a man was throwing sacks into a pit.

"Notice the blemishes on their skin?" said Dad. He pointed to various purple marks on the waxworks' arms and faces. They were round bruises, the size of five-pence coins.

"They've got the plague," said Dad. "It killed thousands in London during the great epidemic of 1665. Very realistic, don't you think? Those sacks the man is handling are body bags. He is the undertaker."

Just then, Dad's pager buzzed. "Got to go," he said. "Some kids are causing trouble at the dodgems. Stay on if you want to. I won't be long."

I didn't fancy staying in the Chamber of Horrors on my own. Not that I was scared, but I didn't like all those eyes following me round the room.

"I'll have another look at the pop stars," I said, following Dad through the tunnel and into the first room.

I heard the door close behind him and looked around me. The waxworks stood silent on their platforms, frozen in position. Suddenly I got the creeps. What if one of the figures moved? I knew I was being silly but I decided to get out.

That's when I heard someone whispering. The noise was coming from behind the curtain in the Chamber of Horrors.

"Hello?" I called out in a hoarse voice.

There was a snigger, followed by a yelp of pain. Someone was messing around in there.

"We're closed," I called out, finding my voice, angry with myself for being so scared.

The sniggering stopped. For a moment there was silence. Then someone started singing in a whisper:

Ring-a-ring-a-roses,
A pocket full of posies,
A-tishoo, A-tishoo…

I yanked the velvet curtain aside, hoping to startle the intruders. But there was no one there except the waxworks, glaring in the flickering light of a lantern…

Chapter Three

Friday, 10.30 pm

I had to stop writing to help Dad make dinner. Now, where was I? Oh, yes…

I was about to let the curtain drop back in place, when I noticed something that made my flesh creep…

One of the kids with the plague had turned his head. He was looking straight at me, his mouth stretched into a horrible grin.

I felt my knees go weak.

"Who are you?" asked a deep voice.

I jumped and nearly screamed. A man was standing in the doorway behind me.

"I'm Becky Soames," I said, "Frank's daughter. You made me jump."

"I'm sorry," said the man, "I didn't expect anyone to be in here. I'm Dario, the owner of the waxworks museum."

He loosened his collar. "It's hot in here. Not good for my babies. The wax might settle."

"Settle?"

"Melt a little," Dario explained. "Sometimes it makes them move. A hand might bend or a head droop under its own weight."

So that was it. The boy's wax had settled. His head had drooped. There was nothing to be scared of.

Except that the boy's head hadn't drooped, had it? It had turned. It wasn't the same thing. Or was it?

"Many of the figures in this chamber are based on real people," Dario said.

I looked at the plague figures. "Even them?"

"Oh, yes," Dario confirmed. "They're based on an old sketch from that period."

"They look real," I said.

"Too real sometimes," laughed Dario. "They even give me the creeps – especially those bullies there. They look nasty."

I turned to look at the boy who had grinned at me. But he wasn't grinning now. His mouth was a thin, lip-less slit across his face.

It was a trick of the light, I told myself. Just a trick of the light.

"We ought to go," said Dario. "Busy day tomorrow." He pushed back the velvet curtain and disappeared. I was about to follow him, when a warm breeze rustled my hair. Something fluttered past my face. It was a faded petal from the bunch of flowers in the fallen boy's hand.

Chapter Four

Sunday, 10.00 am

I have just looked up 'plague' on the net. It was a disease carried by rats. When rat fleas bit people, they became ill and died. By the end of the fourteenth century, 25 million people had died from the Black Death (as they called it) in Europe alone. The greatest epidemic reached London in June 1665.

People burned thousands of rats, hoping to destroy the fleas. But it was too late. A year later, more than 68,000 Londoners were dead. The children started to sing a new nursery rhyme about it:

> *Ring-a-ring-a-roses,*
> *A pocket full of posies,*
> *A-tishoo, A-tishoo,*
> *We all fall down.*

That was the song I had heard at the waxworks on Friday night!

I'm sure there's something weird about those kids in the plague scene, something I can't quite put my finger on. I'm going to go back to the waxworks when it opens again, tomorrow.

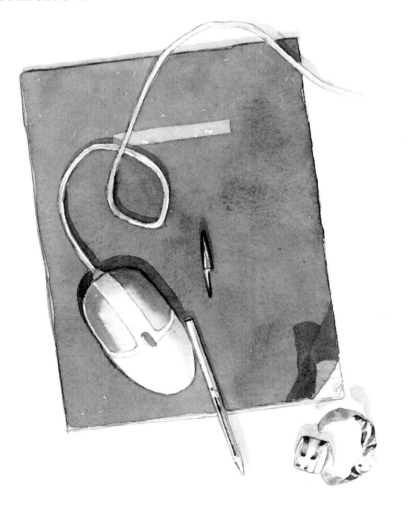

Chapter Five

Monday, 8.00 pm

I'm freaked out. Really freaked out.
Everything seemed normal when I got to the
Chamber of Horrors. Dario had turned the
boy's head back to its original position – at
least, that's what I thought. I'm not so sure
now. I took several photos of the kids
surrounding the boy on the ground. And a
close up of the poor wretch clutching his
precious posy to his chest. He seemed so
helpless, I felt sorry for him. Those eyes…
I'm sure they were filled with tears.

As I clicked away, I wondered why the others were bullying him. Was it just because he was dying of the plague, or did they want something from him?

When I got the photos back from the booth at the end of the pier, I got the shock of my life. There is something in the picture of the boy on the ground that I'm sure wasn't there before. It's a word, a single word, scratched on his bare stomach: *HELP*.

But why does he need *my* help? And what
can *I* do?

There is something scary in the other
pictures, too. The kids aren't looking at the
boy on the floor any more.

They are glaring at me!

Chapter Six

Tuesday, 10.00 pm

That nursery rhyme is really haunting me.
I can't seem to get it out of my head. On
the net I found another website about the
plague. It explained what the song means.

Ring-a-ring-a-roses: the roses weren't flowers. They were the rashes on the victims' skin, just like the marks on the waxworks in the museum.

A pocket full of posies: the posies were meant to purify the air, to keep away disease. That must be what the kids want from the boy – his posy, to ward away death.

A-tishoo, a-tishoo, We all fall down: that's what the other kids fear will happen to them. They'll start sneezing like they have a cold, then they'll all fall down.

Dead.

Now I think I know what kind of help the boy wants from me. He wants me to take away the posy. Then perhaps the bullies will leave him alone. I can't bear to think of him suffering any more. I have to go back and help him.

Chapter Seven

Wednesday, 9.00 pm

There was only a handful
of people in the queue as I
approached the waxworks.
I hung around the first
room, pretending to be
interested in the celebrities
again. When the other
visitors disappeared into
the Chamber of Horrors,
I hopped up on the
platform and hid behind
one of the waxworks.
A bit later the visitors
came back out and slowly
headed for the exit.
I stood in the shadows,
trying hard not to move.
I didn't want to get caught.

Shortly before six o'clock, I heard Dario lock the front door for the night.

I was alone in the dark. Alone with *them*.

A few minutes later I came out from my hiding place. The emergency lights were still on, faint red beams among the still figures.

Gritting my teeth I entered the Chamber of Horrors. My eyes were already used to the gloom, so I focused on the boy lying on the ground. My heart beating rapidly, I hurried towards him. Something brushed against my leg as I stepped on to the platform. I stifled a scream and looked down.

It was a rat made from wax, its eyes glowing like hot coals in the semi-darkness.

I overcame the urge to kick it away and walked right up to the boy. Bending down, I wrenched the posy from his hands. There, I'd done it. Now all I had to do was get out of the place.

All around me, an angry murmur echoed around the chamber. I spun round to see the bullies glaring at me. One of them was pointing at me, his mouth open in a snarl.

I hadn't seen the waxworks move but they were definitely closer to me than they had been a moment before.

"*Get her.*"

I could hear the whisper clearly even though I had not seen any of the waxworks move their lips. Then something poked me in the shoulder and I wheeled round.

The waxworks behind me had moved again. I was surrounded. They were closing in on me.

Someone kicked out the emergency lights and darkness closed around me. There was a scraping sound as waxen feet dragged themselves across the wooden platform. The posy was snatched from my trembling hands. I tried to scream but no sound came out of my dry mouth.

My mind reeled. Then cold, clammy hands grabbed me by the wrist and forced me down to the floor. Something soft and dusty was thrown over my head.

I realized that they were putting me in a body bag.

A flickering light, perhaps it was a lantern, shone through the bag's material.

I panicked and started thrashing out with my arms and legs. But there were too many of them and only one of me. They dragged me along the floor, struggling and whimpering. Someone pushed me hard and I felt myself falling. I'd been thrown in the pit at the back of the tableau. The waxworks were going to bury me alive!

Despair gave me a strength I didn't know
I had. I kicked out with both feet. There was
a hiss as some of the waxworks fell back. My
hands tore at the sack and my nails ripped
through the old material. I scrambled out
of the grave.

The waxworks were waiting for me, the rings on their faces an angry scarlet, growing and pulsating even as I watched.

> *Ring-a-ring-a-roses,*
> *A pocket full of posies...*

They had the posy already. What did they want from me now?

Then a thought struck me like a thunderbolt: *They want your life, your health.*

Instinctively, I kicked out again. Then I saw the boy I had saved. He was standing up. And he was grinning from ear-to-ear. He'd tripped up the kid who had been holding the lantern. There was burning oil all over the floor. The curtains at the far end of the room were on fire.

All around me there were howls of rage and pain. The heat was melting the waxworks.

Then the fire alarm went off and the sprinklers came on. The door to the museum swung open automatically and I darted out to safety.

Chapter Eight

Thursday, 10.00 am

Well, this diary certainly turned out to be more exciting than I'd expected!

My dad once told me that, in the past, some people refused to pose for photographs in case their souls got trapped in the pictures. Perhaps that was what had happened to the children in the waxworks.

Maybe their spirits had been caught in the sketch Dario told me about. And, somehow, a part of their soul had been transferred to the waxworks. I'll never know.

But now they are free, all of them. The blonde boy will suffer no more; the bullies are gone forever.

I wonder if anyone at school will believe my story. And I wonder what I can do to get rid of this bruise-like rash on my arm? The spots are red and round like five-pence coins, and very, very itchy. It looks real but, every time I try to scratch it, the rash disappears…

DARE TO BE SCARED!

Are you brave enough to try more titles in the Tremors series? They're guaranteed to chill your spine...

The Curse of the Ghost Horse by Anthony Masters
Jake believes the ghost tale of Black Bess, a horse that fell to her death when forced to jump a huge crevasse. He is convinced the ghost horse is cursing his family and is determined to jump the crevasse to find Black Bess. But will Jake's obsession lead to his death...?

The Bear Pit by Rebecca Lisle
Jed is always teasing animals. Hester decides to show him the run-down Victorian bear pit so he'll realize how cruel it is. But Jed is fascinated by the pit. When he finds an old leg-iron used to torment the bears, he wants to keep it. But the pit is haunted and the ghostly bears have something else in mind...

The Headmaster's Ghost by Sam Godwin
It's the school trip to Mortimer Hall. Adam and Melissa decide to scare Danny senseless by telling him the story of the evil headmaster's ghost who haunts the house. Danny is determined to show he isn't scared. But does his detemination bring him more than he bargained for...?

All these books and many more can be purchased from your local bookseller. For more information about Tremors, write to: The Sales Department, Hachette Children's Books, 338 Euston Road, London NW1 3BH.